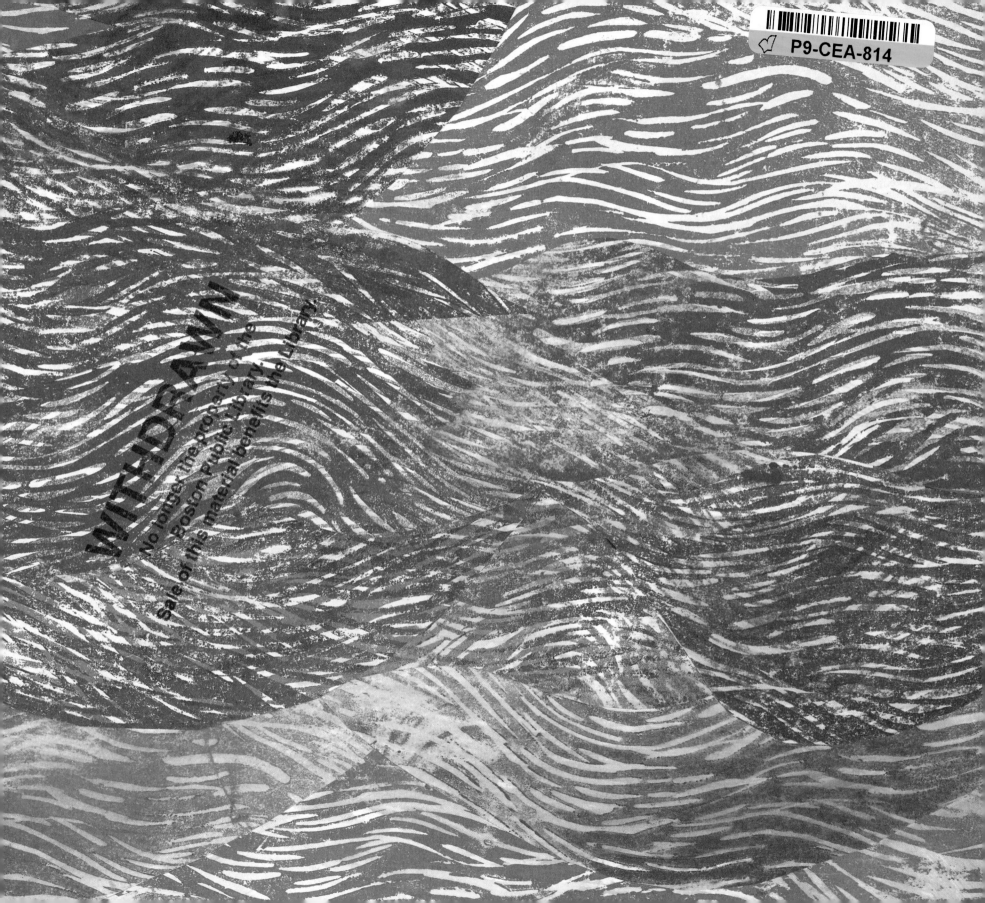

Mrs Noah's Pockets

For Nicola Davies, for the friendship
and the inspiration, always – *Jackie*

For Toto – *James*

Text copyright © Jackie Morris 2017
Illustrations copyright © James Mayhew 2017

First published in Great Britain in 2017 and in the USA in 2018 by
Otter-Barry Books, Little Orchard, Burley Gate, Herefordshire, HR1 3QS
www.otterbarrybooks.com

A catalogue record for this book is available from the British Library.

ISBN 978-1-91095-909-1

Illustrated with collage and mixed media

Set in Berling

Printed in China

9 8 7 6 5 4 3

Mrs Noah's Pockets

Story by **Jackie Morris**

Pictures by **James Mayhew**

Otter-Barry BOOKS

It rained.

Not the kind of rain that comes
in a shower, then passes.

This rain came from a sky
dark as a bruise,
falling hard and fast,
beating the earth,
washing down tracks,
making streams of pathways
and rivers of roads.

Mr Noah stood on a hill,
saw the water rising,
began to build an ark.

"This," he said, "will be the ideal
time to tidy up the world a bit.
The ideal time to get rid of some of
those more troublesome creatures."

By day Mr Noah would draw out plans, hammer and saw at wood, steadily building the biggest boat the world had ever seen.

By night he sat in a corner and made lists, one for all the animals who would sail with the ark, two of every kind, and one for the 'troublesome creatures' that Mr Noah wished to leave behind.

All the time Mrs Noah watched Mr Noah.
She saw the plans. She watched as he worked.
She saw the lists. She smiled.

She took out her sewing machine
and began to stitch.

She snipped and she threaded
and she tacked and she tucked
and she stitched.

'How lovely,' thought Mr Noah.
'Mrs Noah is making curtains
for the windows of my ark.'

Mrs Noah just smiled.

When the ark was finished Mr Noah gathered together
animals from all around the world, two by two,
and took them into the shelter, out of the rain.

Mrs Noah went for one last walk,
wading through water, into the heart of
the Mythico Wood, on errands of her own.

At last all were gathered inside
the ark. It heaved with animals,
large and small. Mr Noah had
been too busy and important to
notice there were no curtains at
the window.

Mrs Noah wore a brand-new coat,
stitched and snipped and tucked
and turned, with a hood and a cape
and very deep pockets.
Lots of pockets.

And still it rained.
The hollows of the land
began to fill. Lakes formed
in valleys. The water rose
higher and higher until it
tickled the base of the boat
where it rested on the hill.

The water lifted it.
    They began to float.
        Mr Noah cut the ropes
            that held the ark
                at anchor
                    and away
                        they
                            drifted.

The rain beat on the roof,
great rods of battering rain.
All the animals and Mr Noah
and the children sheltered in
the dry of the ark.

Mrs Noah stood on the prow,
wearing her hood up, umbrella
in hand, watching the dolphins
and mermaids racing the waves.

Every evening, after all the animals had been
cared for, when the owls began their evening song,
Mr Noah would fall asleep.
Mrs Noah would gather the children around
and tell them tales of dragons and unicorns,
griffin and phoenix, centaurs and jackalopes,
wolpertingers and all manner of things.

Now and again Mr Noah would wake and mutter,
"Bah, unicorns. Troublesome creatures."

The children sometimes thought
they could see things moving,
deep in Mrs Noah's pockets.
Maybe it was just a trick of the light.

Then one morning everyone awoke to silence.
The rain had stopped.
The clouds began to roll away.
The sky was a most beautiful cornflower blue.

Everyone waited, everyone watched as Mr Noah sent out a raven to search for land.

Later that day the raven came back.
No land anywhere.
It seemed that the world had drowned in all the rain.

The ark sailed on. Mr Noah sent out a dove. High, high in the clear blue sky, they all watched until she disappeared.

Much later that day, as the sun coloured the sea to glow with gold, over the water she came.
In her beak was a small twig of green olive.

The next day they followed the dove until the ark
came to rest on the tip of a mountain.
All the animals spilled out onto the land
as Mr Noah watched and smiled. So much
tidier without those troublesome ones.

Mrs Noah, her coat-tails flapping in the
warm wind, wandered away from the ark,
into a wood that grew close by.

Here, one at a time, she emptied her pockets,
being very careful to lift the creatures all out,
setting them free,
two by two,
into the new land.